My Book

Jessica

The First Night of Christmas

Story by
Samuel B. Beardsley

Illustrations by
Margaret Jervis

THE C.R. GIBSON COMPANY
Publishers
NORWALK, CONNECTICUT

'Twas the first night of Christmas,
　　a long time ago,
The hillside was peaceful,
　　the moon was aglow.
The world couldn't know,
　　from what happened before,
That men would remember
　　this night evermore.

The sheep on the hillside,
their day's journey over,
Were dreaming sweet dreams
of a field full of clover.

The shepherds were watchful
while guarding their flock.
The earth was their pillow,
the stars were their clock.

Then all of a sudden,
   they jumped at the sight
Of the sky all ablaze
   with a heavenly light.

They huddled in fear,
    then they started to rise
As the lightning-like flashes
    tore open the skies.

The heavens were split
    by the silvery ray.
The dark disappeared
    and the night became day.
And lo, at the end
    of this rainbow of light,
Appeared then an angel
    to banish their fright.

The angel brought news
    of a birth in a manger
And bade them to hasten
    to welcome the stranger.
For Mary had just
    given birth to a boy,
Whose coming would bring
    so much comfort and joy.

A choir of angels looked down
    from the sky
And heavenly voices were heard
    from on high:

"Peace be on earth
and good will to all men,
The Saviour has come
on this night. Amen."

The heavenly angels
    then faded from sight.
The sky once again
    turned from day into night.
The shepherds all quietly
    rose from the ground,
And hurried to go where
    the child would be found.

As they reached Bethlehem
   and the inn was in sight,
From the barn came a trickle
   of half-hidden light.

It led like a path
        to a soft little bed
And shone very tenderly
        on a child's head.

The child in the manger
    was sleeping so sound,
His eyes were still closed
    as the shepherds stood 'round.

From that instant of grace
    on that night long ago
Thousands of years would be
    warmed by the glow.

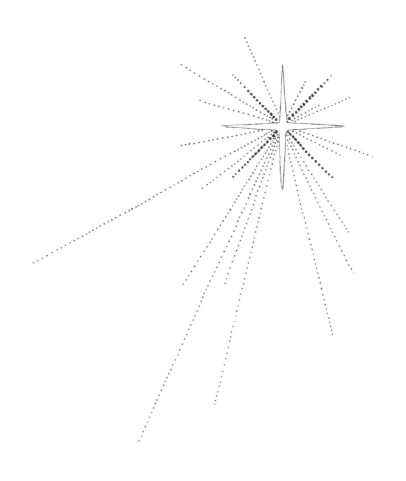

Guided by light
    from a bright shining star
Came a pilgrimage led
    by three kings from afar.

They were dressed in the finest
    of satins and lace.
Their complexions were that
    of an Orient race.

The three wealthy kings
    were wise men and proud
But they went to the Christ Child
    and solemnly bowed.

They came bearing treasures
of incense and gold
To that sweet little child,
still not very old.

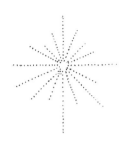

The star in the sky
    twinkled down from above.
The world was awakened
    to kindness and love.

The past was forgotten,
    the future was bright
And the spirit of Christmas
    was born on that night.